DON'S VENDETTA

THE DONS OF WARRINGTON TRILOGY
BOOK 3

ISOBEL WYCHERLEY

Dedicated to Mum & Dad

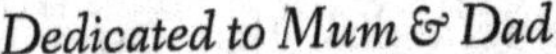

"Revenge is a dish that tastes best when served cold."

DON VITO CORLEONE, THE GODFATHER.

INTRODUCTION

For months now, various Mafia families have been filling our streets with blood. Dubbed World War III, England has been the nucleus for the violent attacks, with billions of pounds-worth of damage being made in the last few weeks.

But at last, families can rest easy tonight knowing that the biggest threat from the Mafia families has been exterminated by our faultless police force. It took months, but one by one, officers picked off the foreign invaders that destroyed our livelihoods.

However, the whereabouts of a handful of Mafia members are unaccounted for, so the force asks for our continued diligence and surveillance of each other; they could be among us.

Baulsack Mafia – DECEASED AND DETAINED
Genghis Li – DECEASED
Anastacia Smirnoff – UNKNOWN
Rasmus Rasmusson – DETAINED
Leon Larsen – DECEASED
Maximus Torrio – DECEASED
Elyasaf Narkis – UNKNOWN

Dobromil Watchoutski – DECEASED
Van De Jaager Mafia – DECEASED
Dionysius Moralis – DECEASED
Paddy Quinn – DECEASED
Gyp Caruso – UNKNOWN
Brock Chadman – DETAINED
Fontana Mafia – UNKNOWN

2

———

SHELLEY

It's been fifty-seven days since the killer got away. I've thought of nothing else since. Not even the breakdown of my marriage, nor being fired from the Met.

The walls of my lonely apartment are papered with documents, clues, pictures of the suspect. I've been chasing a new lead, someone spotted him in Amsterdam last week, but there's been hundreds of so-called eyewitnesses. I've been all over the globe chasing their testimonies and nothing has ever been revealed.

Suspect spotted in casino, Vegas – nothing.

Suspect spotted in Colosseum, Rome – nothing.

Suspect spotted in gorilla cage, Victoria – nothing. *Though there wouldn't be.*

But I can't give up.

Rushing to my computer, I book a ticket to Amsterdam, leaving tomorrow.

Returning to my police radio, hidden in the spare room, I do what I always do every day, simply sit and listen. It's the only talking I hear these days. Never get many visitors. Apart from Reinhold occasionally, but mainly to tell me to let things go, enjoy a peaceful "retirement".

Who does he think he's kidding? The only thing that can stop me caring about this case is a bullet to the head.

A couple of steady knocks at the door interrupt my thoughts. I switch the radio off and cover it with the dish cloth. As I walk through the quiet hallway, the papers on the walls rustle behind me, putting me on edge. I stare at the door behind the safety of the wall. I can see a dark figure through the frosted glass. Swallowing hard, I approach the door.

With my neck pinched in like the wary turtle I am, I open the door slowly, peeking around before it's fully open.

"Hi, Dad," Sonny almost whispers.

I straighten up in surprise. "Sonya, how great to see you! Come in, come in." She looks much older than she did the last time I saw her. *Don't we both.*

She smiles slightly and steps inside, already frowning at all the evidence mounting up on the walls.

"Still looking for him then?" she asks.

"I won't stop until I find him," I reply, closing the front door gently.

I lead Sonny into the living room. "Would you like a drink?"

"No thanks, Dad. I'm only here for a quick visit, I have something to tell you."

I quickly take a seat on the couch in front of her. "What is it?"

"I'm... going to Italy."

I stare at her, waiting for the rest, but she stays

silent. "Oh... that'll be nice, make sure you send me a postcard."

She looks at her feet. "It's not a holiday." She elaborates this time. "Me, Luca and Stefano are going to find Mario." She looks at me again now. "To kill him."

"No, no, no, no, no." I begin pacing the room. "Look what happened to your sister when you got involved with those people!"

"It was Len that killed Al, but Mario is responsible for that."

"I am responsible for that!" I don't know how, but suddenly I am in floods of tears, finally allowing myself to break down.

Sonny wraps her arms around my shoulders. "It wasn't your fault, Dad." Her voice quivers.

"I should never have sent her into that place."

We have had this conversation numerous times, there's no convincing me otherwise. I took her out of a dangerous situation and threw her straight into another one. What kind of father does that? If it wasn't for me, Sonya's sister, Alice, wouldn't be dead, she'd be starting the beginning of her career. I wonder what her profession would be. Stunt woman? Olympian? She'd always wanted to be an interpreter, but I told her to reach higher. She was too clever to recite other people's words, too original.

"You can fight me all you want on this, Dad. I'm going, and I'm gonna kill him, he deserves it. You know this feeling," she tells me, pointing my eyes towards the paper-scattered walls. "I'm not gonna stop until it's over."

After a while, I nod, my bottom lip quivering. "Okay," I whisper, "but be careful."

"You too."

She pulls me up off the floor, and I walk her through the hallway, towards the front door again.

"Are you any closer to finding him?" she asks me.

My bottom teeth grip onto my lip. "I've got a new lead in Amsterdam, I'm flying tomorrow."

"Good luck." She smiles, placing her hand on my shoulder and giving it a gentle squeeze.

"You too." We look at each other with the recognition of pain.

I open the door for her, and she steps out onto the shared landing outside in the breezy Manchester air,

"She wouldn't be happy with us living like this. That's why it needs to end."

I agree, silently.

"I'll speak to you soon, I love you," she says as she turns to leave.

"I love you too, darling."

I slowly shut the door on myself, unsure of how to feel about the interaction. She's so grown up now, she reminds me of my younger self, ambitious and determined.

Part of me doesn't want to dig into this part of her life, we hardly discussed the Mafia since. But I do wonder where Sonny's quest started.

3

———

SONNY

The thing I hate the most, really, really hate with a passion, is how my life went from guns, action, adrenaline, to paying the wages of the biggest arseholes in the paperclip manufacturing industry.

As I sit here, violently smashing the numbers on the keyboard with my finger, my boss calls me into his office.

He's a small man, with wavy brown hair. He either waltzes up and down the office floor, walking on his little tippy toes, making sure everybody's looking at him, or else he's talking loudly on the phone, trying to impress female colleagues: "Oh, you do cardio? That's cute."

Or he's bragging loudly to one of the male co-workers: "Yeah, I had a chick back to my place last night and my girlfriend totally walked in on us. It was so awkward, man."

All of it is fake of, course, you can hear it in his voice, like he's repeating everything he says from the mouth of a main character in a teen flick, or something equally as shit.

"Sonya, your performance this week... less than

satisfactory." He shakes his head with an annoying, condescending, punchable fuckin' look on his face.

I contain my anger but not my distaste. "Okay."

"You see, here at Mr. Clips, we appreciate the value of the small, undervalued paperclip. It holds things together," he explains, demonstrating with his hands. "And you, Sonya, are the paperclip of this company. We need you to work to your best ability."

"I thought my job title was Account Manager, not Paperclip," I remark sarcastically.

He lets out the fakest laugh I've ever heard. "Oh, you've always been a funny one, Sonya." His face drops to a level of contempt I've never seen him display before. "But you're not here to make jokes. You're here to make us money."

"Make money? That's not what I do."

"You know what I mean, cook the books, no biggie." He shrugs.

I hold my tongue for a moment. "Really, is that what I'm here for?"

"Oh, come on," he snorts, "you did a lot worse when you were in the Mafia." He raises his eyebrow at me like a teacher telling a child right from wrong. "You should be thanking me for giving you this job in the first place, you dirty crook."

He takes pleasure in rolling out the last part.

"I'll see what I can do, sir," I reply, getting ready to leave.

"Oh, and don't forget," he calls after me, "you have your monthly review tomorrow, so... don't mess up." He smiles, as a warning.

I reenact his false grin. "I'll try my best."

My face drops to stone as soon as the door is closed behind me. Cheeky little prick thinks he can do whatever he wants with no consequences... Well, I guess he can, his dad's a pretty powerful man and nobody messes with his family, not even the Mafia.

After making the company a hundred extra pounds for the day, I finally head home. (Not that it really was extra, I just found an overpayment that needed sorting out, but he doesn't have to know that before my review meeting tomorrow.)

Pulling up in front of my house, I get the oddest feeling that something isn't right. I take a quick look around before dashing out of my car and in through the front door. I head straight to my room to retrieve my pistol that I keep for emergencies. It's also the only remnant I have of my time with the Fontanas.

As I descend the stairs, I hear quiet chattering.

Who the fuck is in my house?

More annoyed than scared now, I storm towards the voices, finding Luca and Stefano in my kitchen, sitting at the table, drinking coffee.

"Sonny!" Luca stands to greet me. "Thanks for inviting us over," he teases.

I smile at him, his cheekiness reminding me of Al.

"*Mi casa es su casa,*" I tell him.

I give them both a long-awaited hug.

"To what do I owe the pleasure?" I ask them, placing my gun on the table now.

He shrugs. "We just came to check on you."

"No, really." I smirk.

Stefano chuckles to himself. "You can't get anything past this girl."

"I should've known," Luca admits. "We wanted to invite you along to Italy with us."

"Oh, yeah. Going for a nice relaxing beach holiday, are we?"

He inhales deeply. "Not quite. This is not a decision I've taken lightly, Sonny, but we're going over there to kill my brother."

My eyes light up with pleasure. "Say no more, I'll be there."

I can tell he's pleased with my unfaltering loyalty, but also slightly offended that I'm so keen to exterminate a close member of his family. Though, he understands, that's exactly what his brother did to me.

"I knew you would agree to it." Stefano grins at me.

"Who else will be there?"

"Just us, and Gyp."

"I suppose that was all that was left."

"Mmm." He nods sadly. "Elyasaf went back to Israel pretty pronto after what happened."

"I think everybody'd had enough of it all by that point. So much violence for so long takes its toll in the end," I think aloud.

"Agreed. That's why it needs to end."

Suddenly I realize. "But wait, why do you want to kill Mario?"

The thought hadn't even crossed my mind, I was so eager to kill him I just supposed everybody else did as well.

Luca and Stefano share a worried glance.

"You won't have heard about my father," Luca almost mumbles and I struggle to understand him.

"Is he okay?"

"He is now."

4

———

THE DON

1 MONTH BEFORE

Mario returns to the complex alone, prompting everybody in the office, Luca, Sonny, my button men, Gyp and Elyasaf Narkis, to stand alert.

"Where's Al?" Sonny questions.

Mario searches for the right words. "Your father..."

"*Oy vey.*" Narkis sighs, putting his hand to his forehead, already knowing what is about to be said.

Sonny pushes further. "So where is she? What happened? How come they didn't catch you?"

"I don't know, I wasn't in the room at the time," Mario protests, holding his hands up in surrender.

"*Fortunato,*" I mumble, in a way that is cold and unbelieving.

Mario notices.

"What do I do?" Sonny worries.

"I think it is best you resign from your post, *mio amore.*"

She blinks, speechless. "Why?"

I sigh. "It is over, Sonny. We can't risk you being caught too. I suggest you go out and live your normal life."

"How am I supposed to do that? I'm invested in this family now."

"*Invest* in your own family."

She looks sadly at us all, hoping at least one of us would object to her dismissal. Feeling like an outcast and unwanted by us all, without another word she leaves The Complex.

After the awkward and suffocating dust settles, Mario asks the room, "Excuse me gentlemen, may I have a word alone with my father?"

They all look to me, and I give them my approval. They exit the room and Stefano, my confidant, signals to me that he'll be right behind the door. I nod my thanks to him.

"What is the matter, my son?"

Mario sits on the desk, close to me. His knee is basically holding his hand, so that it pushes my palm slightly into the armrest.

"Father... I want to take over from you," he states bluntly.

"Why is that?"

"You're getting old. We need a Don who can be out fighting with the rest of the family."

I stare my son in the eyes calmly. "Is that so?"

"That is so, Father," he replies instantly.

"Well, you needn't worry. A new Don has already been selected for once this war is over."

Mario's eyes light up and he smiles wildly. "Really? Thank you." He laughs to himself, his shoulders bouncing with delight, his head pointing to the heavens. "I knew you'd see the sense in it."

"It's not you, Mario. It's Luca."

His joyous smile turns to confusion, then to a

twisted rage. "What...?" He gawps, "Luca... Luca! Why would you pick him over me?"

"He is smarter, less *impulsivo*. It was an easy choice."

Mario starts to turn red now as his blood boils, and his muscles grow even larger, as if he really will turn into The Hulk at any given second,

"You said you would pick me!" he whines.

He spins my chair towards himself and tightly grips my wrists, strapping me to the chair. "I did not give you my whole fucking life so you could just take it away like that." He speaks in a low growl and I know he's trying to control himself, so he doesn't shout and alert somebody.

"Does Luca know it's him you've selected?" he asks.

"I hadn't told him yet, he knows nothing," I lie, trying to protect my son.

"Good. Now he'll never know."

Steadily, he begins to strangle me. Now weak from Parkinsons I cannot fight back, though I wish I could. I try to call for Stefano but no noise can escape Mario's snake-like coil around my neck. My last resort is to look my son in the eyes as he drains me of life... hope he has a change of heart. But Mario is too furious now, his eyes do not see what is really in front of him.

In shallow breaths the war comes to an end.

Mario

Slicking my hair back into place aggressively, I straighten myself up and look around the office. My mind begins to work properly now, as the dread sets in and my rage settles. They'll know I killed The Don, I'll never be in power in this family now.

I take a look at The Don, dead in his throne, face full of fear. I've never seen my father scared. Never. Not until now. I grimace, partly at my father's cowardice in the face of death, and partly because I recognise that I am the only monster that could extract that reaction from The Don.

I exhale with relief entwined with a rumbling panic. "*Fanculo.*"

I decide it's time to relocate, and I know exactly where to go, exactly who to contact, and exactly who to kill.

Stefano taps on the door quietly. Taking that as my cue to leave, I hurl myself out of the office window and head off to my next destination.

5

———

LUCA

It's hard work getting rid of the mountains of evidence that we've got on these laptops. It's always a strangely melancholic time when a big mission comes to an end, and you must destroy all the hard work that's been the backbone to our success.

I always remember when Papà first introduced me to the family business. I was eighteen, already starting university. I was set to complete a degree in cyber security, a somewhat unheard-of discipline for the time. He'd always ask me what I'd learnt that day, and I was always curious as to why he was so intrigued; he never seemed like a tech-savvy man.

Then, one day, Mario and Vino started to drop hints.

"We could use a cyborg like you in the family business," Mario would joke,

"Yeah, Fonty's is always under cyber threat." Vino would smirk and roll his eyes.

My intelligence led me to the answer I'd been seeking about what our family really did. Well... I say my intelligence; in actual fact, I followed Mario into the saferoom one night and saw everything.

There was no hiding it from me then. Dad sat me down and gave me the option: I could either join them, helping with the technological aspects of the missions, or I could continue my degree, but I would have to leave the country, go and live in Italy with some distant relative.

I don't think he would have made me do that, but instead the threat was meant as a warning – if you decide to join, there's no going back.

My reminiscing is interrupted by screams downstairs. It's a sound I've never heard from Stefano, but his tone is distinct, and it chills me to the bone. I hurry down the stairs and am met with Stefano stumbling down the corridor, like he cannot control a single thing happening to him.

"Stefano, what's the matter, have you been drugged?"

He doesn't hear me.

I grab hold of his sleeves and pull his face towards mine and, in Italian this time, I ask him again, "What's going on!" This is no longer a request – I must know.

The wailing stops, but there are no words. He face is left stuck and drooped in a painful mope.

He can't bring himself to say it. The unimaginable dread he must have felt, being feet away as his lifelong friend is murdered by his son. Behind the door that he himself is guarding, supposedly protecting The Don from harm.

He silently looks over at the office behind him. I can't step over the door frame once I see what's inside. I don't want to get any closer, don't want to see it any clearer, so I quickly take off my glasses.

I think about holding myself together. I must appear strong, as my father always did.

Who is here to care?

Stefano has already broken down. I have no family left here.

I put my glasses in my pocket and gently lower myself onto the floor next to Stefano, my tears threatening to erupt out of my eyes at any second; they're just waiting for that little nudge. That 'little nudge' comes in the form of Stefano dragging my head into his shoulder, and we both weep like babies for hours on end in the cold, empty corridor.

Dehydrated and tired, we finally fall still.

Sniffing, Stefano makes the first move. "I feel better now," he croaks, voice even deeper than before.

I nod viciously, hoping he doesn't say anything to set me off again.

"It was Mario, you know," he tells me, his mouth contorted with hatred.

It does not come as much of a surprise, though I wasn't expecting it, either. In fact, I don't feel anything anymore. There's nothing left to feel.

"What do we do?" I whimper, looking hopefully at him.

"Whatever you wish, Don Fontana."

6

———

MARIO

My journey to Italy starts by smuggling myself onto a cargo train heading to Turin. I survive on the crate of apples that are my travel companions and have pisses through a little hole in the wall; God knows what that looks like from the other side.

I'm not used to this... how do you describe it? Squalor.

All my life it's been first class, chauffeurs, private jets, and now look at me. No better off than a tramp.

Life will be good once I get to Italy, though. There are a few things that need putting in place here first, then I'll return to Manchester in a few days and do what needs to be done, again. *Jeez, why are all the hard decisions left to me?*

I'm gonna start a new Mafia, one where everybody does as I say, or they'll be killed. I'm gonna recruit the teenagers that have nothing better to do or are desperate to provide – *that, sir,* is how you do it right.

I haven't even thought about my dad since; trying to forget about it. Instead, I look forward to the bright future ahead. My own empire, what I've always dreamt of and what everybody knows I've always deserved.

When the train stops, I push myself tight against the door. Some guy, come to unload, opens the carriage door and steps inside. I knock him out with one punch to the skull, or maybe he's dead, who knows.

I jump down from the platform and take in my surroundings. Everybody looks like me... this is great! Rather than sneaking around like I'd suspected I'd have to do, I just stroll on out of there through the main entrance and not one person bats an eyelid.

I come across a nice, secluded road and hitchhike my way to the small village.

"*Grazie!*" I thank my driver, who glides off without recognition.

I take a look at the farmhouses that surround me on the dirt. *I suppose it'll take some getting used to.*

I stride up the uneven stone steps towards the front door and give it two mighty knocks. As I wait to be let in, a beautiful Italian peasant girl enters the street carrying a bucket. She blows a strand of wayward hair from her unblemished skin.

She meets my stare, and smiles shyly at the ground.

God, that's why I love the rural type, so innocent.

The door swings open. "Mario!" Bella chirps, throwing herself onto me.

I laugh and squeeze her tightly. I remember my new lady friend. She's seen this and must have thought Bella is my wife or something, rather than my sister, and she leaves, sadly. I'll explain everything to her later, she will be mine.

"Come in! Everyone's so excited to see you again." She beams, beautiful as always.

The house isn't too bad, actually. Quite nicely decorated. Sitting on the couch in front of the TV is Salva and some random cripple in a wheelchair next to him – he only gets a quick glimmer of my attention.

"Salva, my old friend. How are you?" I grip his hand tightly and we tangle kisses on each other's cheeks.

"I'm good. How are you, happy to be home?"

I laugh. "It's not home just yet."

The cripple moans something loudly and obnoxiously. I frown and whisper to Salva,

"Fuck is this?"

He clears his throat. "It's... Matteo."

"Matteo! How can this be?"

I go in for a closer look. There's nothing to identify him from his former self.

"He ended up in the hands of the Vikings." Salva spits. Literally spits on the floor of his own living room.

"Holy shit..." I proclaim right in front of his face. "And they took a leg."

"They took a fuckin' leg," Salva repeats.

I stand and beckon Salva for a quiet word in the hall and he follows me in.

"Not to sound insensitive, but what the fuck are you keeping him alive for? Look at the guy, that's no way to live."

"He's my fuckin' brother!" He realizes he's talking too loudly and lowers his voice. "I'd be nowhere without him, dead, probably."

"How did you get him back?"

He takes a steadying breath. "They sent him to us," he explains.

"What?"

"They sent him here!" he shouts, as if it was volume that was the problem.

I try to calm him down. "Okay, okay... so, uhh, who's that girl next door?"

He tuts and heads back into the front room where Bella is on her hands and knees, cleaning up his spit from earlier. By the looks of it, he's turned her into a real good little housewife, not what I wanted for my sister but there's nothing I can do about that.

"So," I begin telling everyone, "there's something I need to sort out in Manchester, I'll need to send something in the mail. Is there a post office here?"

"Yes, there's one down the road by the café," Bella tells me. "What are you sending?"

"Great! Just some magazines for my friend." I change the subject quickly, adding, "Oh, and you know what'd be really helpful, Bella? If you could find me a place of my own."

She looks at Salva. "Why me?"

"You have an eye for these things."

"Well, I know there's a room to rent in the –"

"I need two rooms," I interrupt.

"What for?"

I try to hide my smirk. "I have a pal coming to visit."

7

SHELLEY

PRESENT DAY

The girls always said that Amsterdam was such a beautiful place, but to be honest with you, I haven't even taken in the scenery. I don't do anything for pleasure these days, every movement I make has a purpose.

I'm meeting with a guy who replied to my anonymous post about Len. Apparently, he knows something about his whereabouts. We're meeting in a dilapidated building for secrecy reasons, though why he wants to be so secretive I do not know.

I can hear the debris crunching under my feet as I wait, which I seem to be doing a lot of recently. But I don't mind. I always have a clear head, only one goal in life.

The door slides open and a skittish-looking man, no more than five-foot tall, sneaks inside the building to join me.

"You must be Hunter354," I begin.

"That's me." His accent is thick, definitely European but I can't tell what.

"What've you got for me?"

His eyes and feet shift in unison. "I used to work

for this guy, as a driver. He disappears, then reap-pears, off the radar, asks me to pick up his friend."

"What car do you drive?" I interrupt. I can't help it.

"It's a black Maserati."

"That's the car that picked Len up!" I almost scream with excitement. "So it was him, then?"

He becomes sketchy now. "I can't tell you."

"Why not?"

"I will be killed."

"I'll have the police protect you!"

"Please, sir, I know you don't work there anymore, there's nothing you can do for me."

"You have to tell me!"

"No," he says quickly, and begins to leave.

I grab him by the arm and pin him against the wall by his throat,

"If you don't tell me, I'll be the one to fucking kill you."

He looks scared now. "Okay, okay," he trembles, "I know where he is."

"Where?"

"I'll write down the address for you. Len and the other man are both living there, he said."

I let him go. "Thank you."

He leaves before me, and I wait a couple of min-utes before exiting myself.

Now that I have the information that I veed, and I'm getting closer to Len, I allow myself to look around and enjoy being in a new country. The canals really are beautiful, lying beneath the old-style ter-races. *What a narrow country this is.*

Across the road, I see a strange man who looks like he's waiting for somebody. He stands with his back to the water, hands in his deep, saggy pockets. He makes eye contact with me and in a second his eyes widen and he becomes excited. He begins walking towards me.

The ex-copper in me decides it's best I turn around and walk in the opposite direction. He follows me. I pick up speed and so does he. I cut into an alleyway and as he turns the corner, I capture him in an arm control and he squeals, "Hey, let me go, Mistur Shelley, I vant to help!"

"How do you know my name?" I order.

"I know your daughters."

I spin him around. "How?"

"My name ist Bertolt Bertalt ze Sird, I knew you vould be here."

"How?"

Now I sound like a dyslexic owl, great.

"I'm a mystic, I know everysing."

I can't help but roll my eyes. "What do you want?"

"I can help you see sings. Like vhere ze house is."

"What house?" I test him.

"Ze address you have in your pocket. I can show you, so you know vhere you're going."

"How can I trust you?"

"Your daughters did." He smiles reminiscently. "It vas terrible vhat happened to Al, I vant to help."

He can see I'm thinking about it.

"Okay, let's see what you can do."

8

MATTEO

2 MONTHS BEFORE

I had been enclosed in the same room for fourteen days, with no food and little water. Ridiculous really, considering I provided them with useful information they couldn't have procured from anybody else.

The old Victorian house was unusually quiet. It was usually filled with the unintelligible ramblings in languages I do not speak, but that I know are Russian and Scandinavian in origin, but they had seemingly died down.

Somebody came stomping down the corridor and threw open my prison door.

"We are leaving," Anastacia rumbles.

"We?" I frown. "And to where?"

She rolls her eyes. "Not we, me and you. We, me and my associates."

"What about me?" I enquire. "I can go?"

"I'll see what they say," she says bluntly, already closing the door on the last of her words.

"Wait!" She reluctantly reopens the door. "What's happening with the war?"

She seems to soften, dropping her guard, under

what I suspect to be fatigue. "We have lost. I am the only one left."

It takes me a while to comprehend. "So who are your associates?"

"My family from Russia, they're coming to smuggle me home."

"You're leaving my fate to them?"

She pauses. "*Da.*"

This time she really does slam the door.

Maybe I should have asked for food and water, about my brother and my wife, though she's probably run off with the first rich man who showed her any interest. All I had to do was tell her she was pretty and flash my Rolex for her to fall at my feet.

It was perhaps an hour later, though I've lost all track of time now, when the Russian gang returned. I've never been so scared in my life. They're all huge, with meat cleaver hands, a bunch of guys you *really* don't want to mess with.

The leader, a man in a grand ushanka hat and a voluptuous fur coat, strides into the room, his henchmen parting the sea for him.

"*Dobryy vecher.*" (Good evening.)

I look blankly at him. Surely he does not think I look Russian? I have all the generic beauty of a Roman, dark hair, dark skin... class and charm.

"Hello," I reply plainly.

They whisper to each other in their dialect, then the leader asks, "What do you know?"

"About what?"

"About Ana, this side of the war."

I shrug. "I know she's Russian. You've been working with the Chinese, and the Vikings."

"Too much," he cuts in instantly. "Kill him."

He walks out of the room, ignoring my protests.

His bear-like friends close in on me...

First, they stuff my mouth with a dirty rag and torture me by pouring water onto it. I cough and splutter, trying desperately to expel it from my mouth, but they just keep pushing it further down my throat.

They beat me, all over, like a pinata, taking it in turns to join in on the fun. They begin talking; this must've been when they decided what to do with me. They all laugh and one of them returns with a medium-sized wooden crate.

They break all my limbs whilst I'm still attached to the chair. They do this either by hand, or by hitting my joints with a hammer against the chair. I begin losing consciousness but I can still feel everything they do to me.

One of them picks me up and throws me into the box. They all begin pushing and shoving me inside but I won't fit. Another discussion, and they bring out the saw. Rather than take me out of the box again, they just pull one of my legs out and cut it off, using the edge of the box as a table.

I begin to bleed everywhere and their solution for this is to solder my wound shut with a large branding iron. My skin sizzles like cooking bacon, smells like it too.

My protests must've gotten on their last nerve, as they begin beating my head again, until I'm no longer awake.

Now I am left as a vegetable, unable to do anything for myself.

No chance of my wife taking me back now.

If I could move, I certainly would have killed myself somehow, but they attached a sort of rabbit feeder

to my mouth, dripping water down my throat to en-
sure I was still alive by the time I arrived at my destination.

Muffled, from inside the box, I can hear Italian
being spoken, not a dialect I've ever heard before, but
I can make out most of what they're saying. I'm finally
being delivered to my destination.

Staring up at the lid as it creaks open and showers
dust into my crusty eyes, it takes a while for my vision
to adjust. It is my brother, Salvadore. He disappears
for a moment, throwing up against the side of the
crate, before coming back and hauling me out.

He and Bella nursed me as best they could,
cleaned me up and fed me a proper meal, liquid of
course.

Now I sit here, as static as an unmovable boulder,
watching and listening as my brother's life continues
whilst mine hits a tragic brick wall.

God, what did I do to deserve such a fate?

9

————

SONNY

PRESENT DAY

I waltz into my boss' office with the confidence of someone who already knows they're going to quit.

He taps his finger irritatingly on a piece of paper, his small stature making him hardly visible behind the desk.

"Hello, Miss Shelley," he rolls out.

"Hello," I reply, being professional.

"So... It appears you managed to cook up an extra hundred pounds. Unfortunately, that isn't good enough." He shakes his head. "I'm afraid you'll have to stay on late tonight to bring that total up."

"No can do, sorry."

He looks surprised at my rebellion. "No?" He leans back in his chair. "And why is that?"

"I quit."

He blinks as my words process in his tiny pea brain. "You quit?"

"That's what I said," I quip, immediately after.

"You can't quit."

"I can, and I just have."

"You're lucky to even have this job!" His volume increases now.

I scoff. "Well, I wouldn't say lucky."

He doesn't take kindly to the ridicule apparently.

"You'll never get a job like this anywhere else! Unless you're prepared to go back to your sewer rat friends in the Mafia."

I almost tell him that's exactly right, but think better of it; he'd be the first to snitch.

"No, I just have better prospects."

He tries to enact a hearty laugh, hoping for it to be hurtful, but it's so fake even deaf people would've noticed.

"Better prospects, eh? Cleaning toilets, scrubbing floors?"

"It's none of your concern now, is it?" I challenge him.

"You still work for me."

"No, I don't. I just quit." If I'd even bothered to sit down, this is where I would've stood up to leave.

He slides off the edge of his chair, without the use of his kiddie stool, and follows me to the door, stomping angrily like an animated nutcracker.

"If you leave now, you're *never* allowed back in!"

I wipe metaphorical sweat from my brow. "Thank God."

He clenches his fists in a rage and his little gooseberry face turns redder than ever. He shouts whatever it is at the back of my head, but I'm not listening. Except, I did catch the end part: "You should've died with your sister!"

It stops me in my tracks. "What did you say?"

He goes stiff and embarrassed now. A very rare display of speechlessness.

"Go on, say it again, Lord Farquaad," I spit, towering over him now.

Giggles arise from the few eavesdroppers in their cubicles.

He has nothing to say.

"Next time, pick on someone your own size," I tell him, before I walk off again.

I don't think anyone would've intervened if I'd pulled his head off right there and then, God knows he deserves it, but if I ever want, or need, another job, I don't think life imprisonment is the way to go about it.

LUCA

I call my mother where they now live in Italy, on a secure line, of course. We speak together in Italian.

"Hello, Mamma."

"Oh, Luca! It's very nice to hear from you, my love. How is everything at home?"

I'm going to have to share the terrible news earlier than I anticipated,

"Not good, Mamma. Father's dead."

In good old-fashioned Italian tradition, there are no questions, no contradictions, just a deathly howl and floods of tears that I can hear falling onto the receiver.

I take the phone from my ear and squeeze my eyes shut, keeping my own tears at bay.

Once she's regained enough composure, she asks, "How did he die?"

Here comes scream number two.

"Mario killed him."

"NOOOOOOOOOOOOOOOO!!!"

I can't seem to get enough air into my lungs. Why is this the job of a twenty-two-year-old, to tell his mother her husband is dead, and her son the murderer?

"I don't believe it! How do you know it was Mario?" she wails.

"He was the only person with him, Stefano found him alone. Mario's fled but we don't know where."

More crying.

"Mamma, I called you, not only to tell you this, but for advice. I need you."

"What can I possibly do, Luca? I have nothing."

"I need you to tell me what to do. With Fonty's, with The Complex."

"It's over, Luca! Burn it all to the ground!" she screams.

This is useless.

I hang up the phone without saying goodbye and head downstairs, where Stefano and Gyp are talking quietly in the kitchen.

The kitchen used to be the heart of our household. Mother and Nonna would always be in here, cooking all the time, things that smell amazing, that remind them of their childhoods in Roma. Now it is empty and full of sadness. I've never seen it so still or heard it so quiet, it makes my skin crawl.

Gyp makes a big effort with me for the first time ever. He's never understood my importance in the business, of the importance of technology; he was still handling things the old-school way.

"Luca, Luca." He sings my name softly like a lullaby. "Come here, my boy."

If I were perhaps ten years old, this would've been considered soothing and helpful. But as he pulls me in for a hug, I feel nothing. No love, no contempt, no support.

"I want to discuss the business with you both," I tell them as I pull away from Gyp's sweet-smelling embrace.

"We're here." Stefano nods. The look he gives me assures me he doesn't mean just for today, but forever.

We all sit down around the table and I start. "What should I do? With the business, I mean."

"Do you wish to continue wid it?" Gyp asks first of all.

I think about my answer. "I don't know if I'm qualified."

Gyp laughs loudly, it echoes off the walls. "You think anyone'sh qualified for dish? We all catch de bush into Mafia school."

Stefano doesn't join in on the joke.

"I'm only in my twenties, I don't know how to run something like this," I continue.

"You've got ush," Gyp protests, pointing a thumb to Stefano and himself.

"Don't you have your own Mafia to run? You can't possibly help me here, too."

"My Mafia runsh itshelf, shir. I've been in de buishnessh long enough to know how'da do dat, you can have de shame."

I look at Stefano, he shrugs, it's my decision.

Suddenly, something changes in me. I'm no longer satisfied with taking the back seat. I slam my hand on the table,

"Firstly, I'm selling The Complex, or blowing it up, I don't care, but I'm getting rid of it."

Gyp nods, making a mental note of my plans so he can get straight to work.

"Then..."

What then?

"We'll set up a new base. Somewhere nobody knows apart from us three."

"I can do that," Stefano offers.

"We'll keep Fonty's, maybe see if anyone wants to take over so we don't have to worry about it."

Gyp and Stefano nod along.

"Then... we find my brother and we kill him."

They look at each other,

"You're sure?"

"I'm sure."

"Den it'sh shettled."

"Gyp, you can organise staff for Fonty's, and explosives, lots of them."

He sticks his thumb in the air and slides away from the table, not waiting another second to get down to business.

"Stefano, you find a new base. There's someone we need to visit first, though, someone who'll help us with Mario."

He knows who this is, we don't need to say it.

Once we arrive at Sonny's house, it's empty.

"Let's wait inside." Stefano says.

Frowning, I ask, "Do you have a key?"

He reciprocates the confusion. "Do I need a key?"

We pick the lock of the back door and make coffees in the kitchen while we wait. Nice place. She's done alright for herself since leaving, it seems.

She is, of course, shocked to see us, and exccited at the idea of a new mission after months of mundane, normal life.

We will go as soon as we're settled in our new base.

11

REINHOLD

I keep bangin' on his front door but there's no answer. *God, I hope he hasn't died in there.*

"Shelley!" I shout through the letter box.

"Yes?"

He scares the shit out of me, and I bang my head on the door.

"What are you doing?" I shout, rubbing my head.

"What am I doing? You're the one staring through my letter box."

"Was that... humorous?" I gasp. He's not joked in months.

He smiles, but only slightly. "Sure."

He puts his key in the lock and lets us both in. "What are you doing here?" he asks me.

He drags a small suitcase that was sitting by the door, through the hall and shoves it quickly into a small storage cupboard.

"Been on holiday?" I ask him curiously.

"I asked you first."

"I came to tell you that The Complex was obliterated. The Met's over there looking into it right now."

He turns around to face me in the hall. "Was anybody hurt?"

"No. Nobody was there."

He breathes a sigh of relief. "Do you want a cup of tea?"

"Sure."

We go into the kitchen, and he starts on the brews right away, so I take a seat on the sofa.

"So, what've you been up to?" I question.

"Not much." Blunt and secretive as always.

"What's the suitcase for?"

He turns to face me, his back to the boiling kettle. The steam rises and creates a wing behind him, frail and broken. "Am I under interrogation?"

I hold my hands up in defence. "Just interested in what you've been up to."

"Keeping an eye on me more like." He turns around to continue his brewing.

I sigh. "I would be lyin' if I said I wasn't worried about you, Tim. But you seem happier today, that's what I'm interested in."

He pushes a mug over to me across the grubby counter, which is overflowing with letters and unopened envelopes. The mug is crusty, like it hasn't been cleaned properly in a long time. I watch where I'm putting my mouth.

"I finally feel like things are going in the right direction." He nods.

"Really?" I'm surprised to hear something positive come out of his mouth for a change.

"Yeah." But quickly, he changes the subject. "Do you know of anyone called Bertolt?"

I can't help but laugh. "Do I look like a Herr Reinhold to you?"

He shrugs. "Just wondering."

"Do you know a Bertolt?"

"I met him a couple of days ago."

"Oh, yeah? Who is he?"

"He's a mystic."

"A mystic?" I scoff. "What you doin' with a nutter like that?"

He chuckles, again another rarity these days. "I thought the same at first, but he showed me things. I believe it, I believe in him."

"What did he show you?"

He looks sullen now. "Nothing."

"Okay." If he doesn't wanna talk about it I won't make him. "Are you planning on seeing him again?" Perhaps he's using him as a palm reader or something.

"Yes, we're working on something together."

"What're you workin' on?"

I think my questions get too much for him and he starts to feel suffocated, as he suddenly blurts, "I have a lot of things to do today, maybe it's best if you go."

Fine by me. I was a little worried about what I'd find at the bottom of that mug, anyway.

SHELLEY

Bertolt takes me back to the shabby old hostel he's staying in for the night, so that he can show me what he knows about where Len is. It's like a crack den in here; if I was still on the force, I'd have a field day. People are taking drugs in the corridor and dealing them out in the open.

"Don't let on zat you're a cop," Bertolt whispers to me.

I guess he's noticed the other residents eyeing me up, probably due to my distasteful glances at them. We get to his room, which is also thirteen other people's room.

"Are we really gonna do it here?" I ask, feeling very vulnerable about being hypnotised in a public space.

"*Ja!* You vill be fine." He smiles, actually making me feel better.

There's something about him that puts me at ease, like he already knows everything about me anyway, so I don't have to worry.

He sits me on the bed and begins pulling potions

out of his bag like the BFG, mixing them all into a small bottle.

"Drink zis." He passes the glass vessel to me.

He pulls out his bongo drums and sits on the floor in front of me, staring up with an excitable face like a puppy waiting for a treat.

"What are they for?" I nod at the drums on his lap.

"For ze rhyzem." He waves his arms about like tentacles. "Now drink and cloze your eyes!" he snaps, good-naturedly.

I nod, take a deep breath, thinking about whether I really want to do this or not.

I do, there's no other option, Tim.

I squeeze my eyes shut and shot the liquid. It tastes rancid and I almost spill it straight back up. I make the effort to take deep, steady breaths, knowing it won't take much to set me off and plunge me into a debilitating anxiety attack, brought on by the ludicrous situation and my helpless feelings inside.

He begins rhythmically pounding on the drums, it's very relaxing. It's easier to breathe now, almost as if my lungs are contracting themselves, forcing the air through my body in a beautiful, gentle stream. The darkness of my eyelids begins to swirl, and a blurry picture presents itself.

There's a dirt road, forever changing and stripping its layer in the authoritative breeze – I can hear it, whistling in my ears. It's very quiet here, must be in the countryside. The houses are made of wood and uneven stone bricks, it doesn't look like England...

"Hoh-hoh-hoh, duuuuuhd, you have got to get me on this!"

I begin to blink as the image dissipates from my eyes,

"*NEIN!* You have ruined ze trance!" Bertolt shouts at the stoned-looking surfer dude leaning over me.

"Woah, duhd, chill out, bro." He struts away backwards.

Bertolt turns back to me. "Do you sink you can try again, Mistur Shelley?"

"I'll try," I say, closing my eyes again.

Bertolt begins drumming again but nothing appears, the moment is gone,

"No luck." I pout.

He sighs too. "Hmm. Ve can try again later."

"Why not now?"

"It doesn't vork like zat."

"Well, can't you just tell me where I need to go, then?"

"It doesn't vork like zat, eizer."

"Then how *does* it work?" I start to lose my patience now.

He bites his bottom lip as he thinks. His eyes glaze over as he pictures something in his head. "You vill get zere, Mistur Shelley, trust me." He smiles mischievously.

"How do you know?"

Instead of tapping his nose, like a normal person telling someone to keep their beak out, he taps his temple, implying he knows everything. I'll take what I can get, even if it does come from a lunatic's brain.

"Take my number, Mistur Shelley. Vonce it becomes clear, call me and ve vill go," he instructs, handing me a small scrap of paper with a phone number on it.

"You can call me Tim," I say reluctantly. I want to build a rapport with this guy.

He shakes his head. "Al says you only said zat to build... vat? How do you say? R...a...p...oar...t. I don't know, she speaks better Engleesh zen me," he concludes.

"*Al?* Are you playing some sick game with me?" How dare he bring my dead daughter into it! The mere mention of her name, whether good or bad, infuriates me.

He looks shocked. "*Nein*, sir, *nein!* I hear her talking to me."

I do not look impressed.

"Vait! Al... Vhat is somesing I can say to your fazer so he believes me?" His eyes dart above his head like she's a fly buzzing around his ears. "She says, your electricity bill ist srough ze roof and you should probably switch your radio off vhen you leave for zis amount of time... Vhat?"

"How do you know this?"

"I don't know zis, Al knows zis. She vatches you all ze time."

I laugh, because if I didn't, I'd cry. "I don't believe you."

"Vhen your prefrontal cortex is back to normal, ve vill conduct zis again. I vill show you ze house and I vill show you ze rest, also."

I get on my return flight back to Manchester a couple of hours later. I go straight to my police radio to find that the towel has been removed and it's switched on, and the dial has been moved to the frequency 120398, Al's birthday.

I do the only thing I can think of doing, and that's run. I run for miles, away from what, or to where, I don't know, it's just a feeling that comes over me.

I rest at a duck pond to catch my breath. I slump into the bench and look up at the sky, listening to the crowd of quacks skimming on the water. One of them sounds exactly like someone saying 'dad', I look around, startled, but it's only me and the ducks there.

I must be going crazy.

I head back to my apartment and see Reinhold's arse sticking out my letterbox,

"Shelley!" He beckons.

"Yes?"

We go inside and he informs me that The Complex has been bombed, and I can't wait to get him out of the apartment so I can listen for any reports on my radio.

As soon as I finally manage to get rid of him, I head straight to the spare room. It kills me to change the frequency away from Al's birthday, but it needs to be done.

The reports say no signs of life or bodies have been found and nothing remains of the buildings or anything inside them. Thank God Sonny wasn't in there.

This must have been planned. They got everything out and blew it up themselves to cover their tracks... But I can't lose time thinking about this; I'm getting closer and closer to Len.

I unfold the piece of paper in my pocket, smoothing it out on my desk. I quickly, but accurately, type out the address into the map on my laptop.

It pinpoints a small village surrounded by greenery. It looks really out of the way and will be a challenge to get to by commercial travel. Hopefully Bertolt knows what he's doing.

I start to scour the local newspapers of the area; nothing interesting, mostly articles about a fruitful harvest this year and a cow that's pumped out a record amount of milk for the area. Then I come across one about a man, killed in the one of the trainyards, under unusual circumstances. This has to be Len!

I track the journey of the train in questions and discover it took off from Manchester, but a few days before Len was even released. Fuck, another dead end.

ANASTACIA

"I 'm telling you, he's still alive!" I protest.

"Don't be ridiculous, Ana. Even if he survived the journey, there's no way they would keep him alive in that condition."

I huff frustratedly. "I've got intel on him, he's alive."

"Until I see conclusive photographic evidence, this is of no concern to me," my father grumbles.

"Then I will get you your evidence!" I challenge him.

He looks unconvinced, a wise father wishing his little girl would just run off and play spy like she always does.

I'll show him.

I get straight onto the phone to contact a woman I know in Italy, my own little project. She's how we discovered the Russos' new hideout, long ago when Salvadore and Bella first moved there. We've been watching them longer than they know.

"Maria?"

"*Si?*"

"Is *Radicchio* still living next door to you?" (That's the codename we gave him.)

"Um, I have not seen him in long time, but yes, I think he is still there."

"Take a picture of him for me."

"I'm not sure…"

She still doesn't understand that she must do as we say or she will be killed before she can even blink, *Дурак*. (Fool.)

"You will. You will send it to me *on the phone we gave you*," I emphasise, "using *the money we give you* for your continued cooperation. Understand?"

"Yes, ma'am."

"Great. Goodbye."

"Wait!" I hear her shout through the receiver.

I roll my eyes expecting her to ask me for something. "What is it?"

"There is another man here now."

"Who?"

"I don't know, but he looks Italian. Maybe a brother, a cousin?"

"Talk to him, let me know what you find out."

———

A few hours later, our little *spia* (spy) sends me a photograph of Matteo, as well as a picture of her and the mystery man. My father will be beside himself once he finds out. I take the evidence straight to his office, and order his guards to leave.

"What is this about, Ana? I'm very busy."

"Here's your photographic evidence." I throw the two printouts onto his desk.

He looks at them and an evil smirk grows from his small, serious mouth.

"You're going to Italy, my darling."

———

I bet you're wondering why we're bothering with the Italians, especially since their Mafias are basically extinct now. But Matteo was a mistake, we didn't think he'd survive, and now he has the knowledge to catch us out. Luckily for us, he has no way to communicate, but it is still too risky for us for him to be alive.

Mario, similarly, is a threat. Is he the one who blew up The Complex, his family buried deep inside? He is preparing a new age of Fontanas and we cannot let that happen. Not if we want to take over the world without any hassle.

My father decides that I will pay them a visit, to exterminate them once and for all.

14

MARIA

My hands are trembling when I put down the phone. *How will I ever get a picture of him?*

I have to cover my fear, and get the job done; it's not often a farm girl like me gets to join in on exciting adventures like spying.

With a deep breath, I storm through the house towards the front door. When I swing it open, the new man is already on my doorstep.

He looks startled but happy to see me. I soften my expression for him.

"*Salve.*" I smile coyly.

"Hello, beautiful." His teeth sparkle in the sun. "I was just coming to introduce myself. My name is Mario." He takes my hand and kisses it gently, looking into my eyes,

"I am Maria."

"Ah, that'll be easy to remember, then."

This makes me giggle. I can already feel myself coming to like him. This is not good considering Anastacia's interest in him.

"Would you like to come for a drink with us?" he invites me.

I can't believe my luck!

"Yes, please." I beam.

He looks happy for me to be joining him.

He takes me into the small garden. The little grass they have is brown, dried out from the relentless heat, but the rest of the garden is beautiful.

"Do you tend to the garden yourself?" I ask him.

"No, no, my sister, Bella, tends to the house," he explains.

I nod in silent recognition of this new link to who he is.

"Would you like to meet her?"

"Great! I would love to meet everybody here. I have only seen them from afar but we have lived next door for some time now."

"I'll go and get them for you. Are you okay with wine?"

"*Sì, grazie.*"

Soon enough, the whole ensemble is out in the garden. Bella first; she greets me warmly and I gush over how beautiful and stylish she is, even covered in flour from making the evening meal. She is modest and returns the compliment.

Then Mario, clutching a bottle of wine and amazing crystal glasses, not like the ones you see around here. Finally, Matteo arrives, pushed outside in his wheelchair by his brother.

"This is my brother, Matteo. I'm Salva, we met briefly when we first moved here."

"Yes, I remember," I say, taking his hand. "Hello, Matteo."

He groans in reply and, even though it has no linguistic value, the tone of it, it's like he knows what I'm doing here.

We drink for hours, and once I consider everyone to be in good spirits, I ask the million-dollar question. "Can we take a picture together? My cousin sent me a camera phone from Roma, I must use it."

"Sure!" Mario obliges.

Bella is up out of her chair straight away, revelling in the girly nature, which she hadn't experienced in a long time, being stuck inside with two men.

Salva doesn't look too impressed, but joins in on the fun, so Bella doesn't think he's a *guastafeste.* (Spoilsport.)

We all crowd into the screen, and around Matteo, and I snap the picture.

This was easier than I thought.

A few minutes later, I excuse myself to go to the bathroom. As soon as I lock the door, I'm straight on the phone to Anastacia, sending her the evidence she wanted as quickly as possible. Hopefully, it's good enough for her to send me some more money; Mamma hasn't been well recently, and I'm too busy helping Papà on the farm to look after her, so we could really do with the extra help.

I head back outside. It suddenly seems a lot darker than when I first left the table, but everybody is still there, laughing and having a good time.

"I think it's best I head home now," I confess.

Mario's arms stretch out beside him. "You basically are home, my dear. Stay for another drink."

"I can't," I refuse, "my mamma will be worried."

"MAMMA!" Mario shouts drunkenly. "*MARIA STA BENE!*" (Maria is okay.)

Bella stifles her laughter and shushes her brother. "I'm so sorry, Maria, ignore him." She rolls her eyes, a sister who has put up with him for years.

"I'll walk you home," Mario offers.

I chuckle. "It will take me five seconds to get there, you don't have to do that."

But he's already up from his chair, swaying towards me. "I have to protect such a beautiful woman."

He's flirting with me, but when he's drunk, his words don't have the same charm, I realise.

In a few steps, we're at the foot of the stairs that lead up to my front door. "Well, goodnight," I say, hand on the doorknob, ready to leave.

"Don't I get a goodnight kiss?" He smirks, hanging from the railings like the world's weakest sloth.

I pity him. "I don't think so."

"Oh, go on!" he says, pulling himself closer to me and grabbing my arm.

"Mario, I said no." I start to panic now.

"What's that? I can't hear you." His idea of a joke, I suppose.

Just in time, my father almost drags the door off its hinges. He is the biggest man in our village, he is nicknamed *il toro* for the sheer size of him. He has deep eyes, full of sorrow since Mamma got ill, but full of passion. A well-cropped dark beard and matching hair, usually full of sweat from his hard day of labour.

"*Cosa sta succedendo?*" (What is going on?) he asks flatly, staring menacingly at Mario. "*Chi è?*" (Who is he?)

"*Nessuno, Papà.*" (Nobody.) I try to push us both through our door and away from Mario, but he won't budge.

My father tells me to go inside, quickly, and in a way that I know he's going to hurt him. Mario is clearly too drunk to even read the room, let alone decipher Italian right now.

"Oh, come on, Daddy. We're just having some fun," he wheedles.

That's enough for Papà to punch his lights out. Mario tumbles backwards down the stone steps and finally comes to a halt in the dirt. He groans and holds his hands around his head, waiting to see which place hurts the most.

"Stay. Away," Papà warns, in his miniscule knowledge of English.

He closes the door between us, but I peek out of the small window next to the door, looking at the crumpled heap.

"I'll never stay away from you," he mouths quietly, still in pain, lying on the dusty ground.

Fantastic.

15

——————

SONNY

Stefano picks me up in his Alfa and takes me to the new hideout where Luca is waiting for us. As I descend the narrow staircase into the bunker, I can hear Luca singing along to *Tu vuò fa l'americano*. He must be in good spirits today – the day we plan to kill his brother.

I waltz into the room, joining in with the singing, shortly followed by Stefano, and we serenade each other:

> *Tu vuo' fa' l'americano*
> *mericano, mericano...*
> *ma si' nato in Italy!*
> *sient'a mme: nun ce sta niente*
> * 'a fa'*
> *ok, napulitan!*
> *tu vuo' fa' ll'american*
> *tu vuo' fa' ll'american!*

The record crackles as the song finishes, the last track on the vinyl. We all laugh and smile at each other, almost like we don't know what to do next.

"It was my father's favourite song," Luca remembers.

At least he's still smiling, he must be feeling better about it all now.

"Don't blame him, it's a tune," I reply.

This makes him chuckle. "It is."

"This place looks great, by the way; I like that picture," I say, pointing to the one above the dining table.

It's a black and white shot from World War Two, D-Day, of the soldiers preparing to depart from the boat. The fluffy white waves lurch above the lip of the craft, and although you can only see the back of their helmets, you can feel their terror and the wish that these waves were the only thing they had to fight.

"You wouldn't think they sell these in furniture shops, would you?" Stefano wonders.

"Really?" I ask, surprised.

He shrugs. "People are into weird things these days, I guess. But I thought it would be a nice backdrop for our own victory."

"Agreed," Luca states, staring up at it, hands behind his back like a thoughtful old man. "Anyway," he interrupts himself, "let's begin with our planning."

Stefano takes the floor. "Gyp said the plane is ready, it's on the runway right now. But he won't be coming with us."

"Why not?" I ask.

"He's going back to the States for a while, he says it's to plan something *big*, but I think he's scared."

"Scared of what?"

"I don't know," he begins. "Maybe killing Mario, or maybe he thinks Brock will snitch on him soon — he's been locked up for months now."

Luca looks worried. "So Gyp's left us?"

"For now," Stefano replies bluntly.

Luca sighs and bites the inside of his cheek. The start to his reign isn't going very well considering there's only two henchmen left.

"Fuck him!" Luca surprises everybody with his outburst. "Let's get started."

He unveils a map of Italy. A little red cross marks the spot where Mario is living,

"How do you know he's there?" I ask.

"Because he's an idiot," Luca says flatly.

Stefano turns to me to explain further. "He kept his phone, obviously all bugged."

"Gave himself away. Thanks, Mario, you've made our job much easier."

We all crowd into the arms room at the back of the bunker. Piled floor to ceiling with every kind of weapon you can imagine, it's like a gangster's version of a kid in a toy shop.

"I think we should mount something to the plane," I say, without thinking.

Why did I say that?

"Like a machine gun?" Stefano asks.

I shrug. "Yeah, I just think we should have some form of aerial protection, just in case."

Luca nods. "We'll do that. Good thinking, Sonny."

I smile a little bit. It's been a long time since I've been praised for a good idea.

Luca hands me a small mobile phone. "I know we'll be together, but just in case, I want you to have this back."

I take it from him and hold it in my hand. It's the one I got the first time we met. I unlock it, using the same keycode, and the background is a picture of Al and me, in our suits, back-to-back, fingers in the shape of guns, taking the piss out of secret agents.

I laugh and cry all at once. The sounds just fall out of my mouth, and my eyes for that matter.

Both of them hug me, one either side.

"We do this for Al, and for my father," Luca states, his cheek obstructed by the crown of my head.

———

Stefano clips the last piece of the gun onto the side of the plane. He and Luca will be pilot and co-pilot, while I'm given gun duty. Which is probably for the best, since I've never flown a plane.

Then again, I don't remember Luca or Stefano ever flying a plane, either...

"Do you know how to fly?" I ask,

They're busy flicking switches that insulate the cockpit, like icicles forming in the snowman's cave, melting and spreading further across the surface with each icy breath.

"No, but how hard can it be?"

I frown. "Probably pretty hard."

Luca turns in his seat to look at me. "Would you be giving Al this jip?" he says, smirking.

"And then some."

He laughs. "And she'd give it right back. So, shut the fuck up and let me learn how to fly."

I do a small salute. "Copy that," I say down the headset microphone, in an American accent, so it comes out deep and powerful through the speakers.

"Right..." Luca begins, feeling like all the right switches are where they should be. "Does that look about right to you?" He turns to his co-pilot.

Stefano shrugs, looking slightly worried.

"Ladies and gentlemen, my co-pilot's given me the all-clear for take-off. Please fasten your seatbelts as we will be hitting the runway soon, and who knows if this thing'll actually fly."

A few more flipped switches and the pull of a lever and the plane whirls up, its front propeller beginning to spin faster than the eye can comprehend.

"This looks promising!" I shout over the noise of the violent wind we're creating.

Luca messes around with the control wheel and the plane slowly starts to move in delayed motions.

We're all surprised, especially the pilot.

Steering towards the runway, the plane begins to pick up speed. Once we're on the straight, we can feel the wheels desperately trying to pick the weight up off the ground.

"Come on, you prick!" Luca wrestles with the mechanics.

The end of the runway is getting closer and closer and the plane is no further to being in the air.

"Pull up, Luca!" Stefano panics.

"I *am* pulling up!"

The chain link fence advances at top speed. *How embarrassing, we're all going to die and we didn't even get off the runway.*

The plane finally tips and it's fully off the ground, but the wheels catch on the top of the fence before they can neatly tuck themselves underneath the plane. The wheels are ripped off, sending the plane spinning uncontrollably in different directions as Luca struggles to tame the mechanical beast.

After a few seconds, *that feel like hours,* the plane levels and everything seems relaxed.

I imagine the seatbelt lights would go out round about now. Followed shortly by the tea and coffee trolley. *I'll take a tea, milk, one sugar, and one of those scratch cards, please, my love.*

A nervous laugh fills the cockpit as we all realise we've somehow pulled it off.

"See, I told you, Sonny. Easy," Luca jokes.

"Mmm," I concur, "I especially liked the part where the wheels came off."

Stefano chimes in now. "Who needs wheels, anyway? It's not like we're going to have to land safely."

Nobody had thought about the landing yet. *Shit.*

"We'll be fine." Luca hesitates, then adds, "Parachutes in the back if we need them."

I do indeed think we'll be needing them.

Now that we're steady, I unbuckle myself to gawp at all of the controls on the panel.

"What's that?" I point.

"How am I supposed to know," Stefano mopes. "Do I look like a pilot to you?" he asks, sat in his co-pilot chair, nothing but empty sky ahead of him, all he's missing is the hat.

"Ya." I nod.

"Oh." He coughs and grumbles, taking the manual out of its sleeve. "It's the *altitude indicator,*" he reads.

I point to the next thing. "That's the radar, isn't it?"

"I think so."

"Then what's that?" I point to the little green dot on the display, travelling at the same speed, towards us.

Luca and Stefano join in to squint at the screen,

"Looks like another plane," Luca reckons.

Simultaneously, we all look out of the window and see that ahead of us, a similarly small plane is gliding smoothly in our direction.

We stare in wonderment for a moment, taking in the beauty. Until we see that it isn't diverting, and neither are we. We're gonna crash head-on.

I push the control wheel to the left, an action forced out of me by life-threatening adrenaline, and the planes miss each other by inches. I get thrown into the back of Stefano's seat, but it's not as bad as it could've been.

The other plane expertly manoeuvres itself around and begins to close in on us from behind now.

"Oh no, are we gonna get pulled over for reckless flying now?" Luca asks, half joking, but half believing in the air police.

But it's much worse. A barrage of bullets fire at our plane, miraculously dodged by Luca, who swings the plane from side to side in his panic and I rush back to my seat in the rear of the plane to get a better look.

Grabbing the binoculars tucked into the seat pocket, I try to hone in on our enemies.

Fuck off. "It's Anastacia!"

"What?" Luca and Stefano shout, both bewildered.

"What the fuck is she doing here?" Luca spits.

"Tryna kill us by the looks of it, mate," I reply casually.

More bullets fly past our windows and ping off of God-knows-what, sounding like a wasp on speed.

"Sonny, I'm gonna get us in a good position, let 'em have it," Luca instructs.

"Yes, sir." I get into position, strapping myself into the chair and getting a tight grip on the gun's handles.

Our plane takes a quick right and I come face-to-face with theirs. Without aiming, I keep hold of the trigger and hope that just one slug hits a major artery. But it doesn't.

"Go round again!"

The Russians are on more of a kamikaze mission. Their plane edges dangerously close to ours and I'm sure I hear the wing of theirs connect with our rudder.

"I think this may be your last chance, Sonny," Stefano manages to say, after a quick and desperate prayer.

Once again, I'm in position, I really can't fuck it up this time. Everything becomes so clear all of a sudden. I can see the face of the pilot, Anastacia next to him, a determined grin on her face. *You bitch.*

I hold the trigger with all my might, as if its power and accuracy depended on how hard I could push it down. Like an explosion, when one bullet hits, the whole plane twitches and erupts with fire.

Their plane starts to lose altitude (*which would be displayed on their altitude indicator*) and their faces are no longer visible behind the cloud of smoke and flames. Suddenly, it drops, as if losing power all at once, and the battle is over, just like that.

An anticipatory silence falls within the cockpit once more,

"Are they gone?" Luca croaks, his throat too dry from his fear.

"Yeah," I say, through a relieved breath of air.

Stefano clears his throat. "We're only ten minutes from the landing strip now, what are we going to do?"

The panic returns. *Thanks for reminding us of that, Stefano.*

We put the parachutes on, just in case, though it'd probably be too late to use them once we realised a landing wasn't possible.

Another quick prayer from Stefano and we begin our descent. Luca slowly drops the plane into a less drastic nose dive.

"Drop the wheels." I say, trying to break up the tension with a bit of comic relief.

It gets ignored, probably bad timing, and because it's in poor taste.

"Ah, fuck it." Luca gives up trying to land. "We'll never make it, let's just jump."

"Are you sure?" Stefano panics; he's scared of heights.

Luca looks around to me. "Sonny?"

"I'll jump."

"Come on then."

The pilots both leave their stations, and the plane begins to fall rapidly now. Luca grabs the rucksack full of everything we need before teetering on the edge of the aircraft.

"On three!" Luca shouts.

"Three!" Stefano jumps out of the plane before the count even begins.

Luca and I follow shortly after, not wanting to waste any more time staring at the floor we're about to collide with.

I fall at a higher speed than the other two, and I've caught up with Stefano's fall in no time. Unfortunately, we both activate our parachutes at the same time and the ropes become tangled, sending us both on a carousel of terror.

We both struggle desperately to untangle our chutes, but it's no good, the force and speed of the fall makes it impossible to control any sort of movement.

"I'll cut my ropes!" Stefano informs me, reaching into his pocket for a knife.

"Stefano, no, we'll fall together, it'll be fine!"

He begins hacking away at the pressured rope, its individual threads pinging away from the central structure, fraying out one by one *like the hairs on the back of my neck.*

We're getting dangerously close to the ground now. I've stopped protesting to Stefano. Part of me wants him to cut it, so at least one of us can survive, but the other part desperately loves the gentle giant and I know how much he means to Luca.

The rope snaps and Stefano plummets away from me, my chute finally opening and bringing me to a gentle, steady descent. *Weightless.*

Something – a bird? – races past me, sending a gust of wind down onto my life-saving canopy. It's Luca, who's yet to release his chute. He grabs hold of Stefano, by some crazy fuckin' miracle, and pulls the chord just in time for a not-so-devastating landing against the hard dusty ground.

Our plane falls dangerously close to me in the air, I can feel the heat of the engines swirling around in the parachute. I've never seen a plane crash from above. It's not as dramatic, more like dropping a toy and watching the pieces splay out across the floor.

The fire was cool, though. Thankfully, Luca and Stefano were far away enough not to be covered by the fiery blanket.

I reach the floor and they're both groaning in pain, spread-eagled in the middle of nowhere. The air is humid and stings with the smoke from the plane crash, and the sun beats down like a steady drum on my face.

It looks like Stefano's broken his wrist, he's holding it tightly in his other hand, but he's keeping himself together.

"Are you alright?" I rush over to them, kneeling down in the powdery dirt.

Stefano coughs; the chalky particles that cover his face and body shoot out of his moustache into the still, hot air,

"I'm okay," he rasps.

"Luca?"

"I'm okay, too... Stefano broke my fall."

All three of us can't help but laugh at this; we've escaped death more times today than we'd like to admit.

16

———

LUCA

I rip a section of the parachute off and wrap it around Stefano's broken wrist. "It's not much, but it'll have to do for now," I tell him.

He smiles at me. "Thank you. I understand."

What an amazing guy he is.

"What now, boss?" Sonny asks.

I pull the tracker locator out of the rucksack. "We find him." I wiggle the device in front of her. "He's not too far from here. Maybe we can get a taxi or something."

We all look around, there's nothing but desert and trees.

"Reckon they do Ubers up here?" Sonny adds sarcastically.

"We better start walking."

I dust myself off, finally looking more human than the ghost I was before, covered in all that grey sediment. I hand out the bottles of water from the bag; they get drained almost immediately by everybody.

In the distance, we spot a farmer riding his horse, dragging along something that looks like (*and, even if it isn't, we'd use it as*) a carriage.

Sonny, the one of us with the best health, runs over to him to ask for a lift into whatever town is nearest.

He obligingly picks us up and we sway painfully on the back of the wooden crate, feeling every tiny stone underneath the old, battered wheels. He makes no effort to hold a conversation, which is fine by us all, taking the journey time to think about what's ahead and what's just happened. *In all of its glory.*

He drops us off about twenty miles away from where we landed, a small market town full of fruit and dairy stalls and farmers chattering to each other, the only people they've ever known. I look at the tracker again, and the dot is within walking distance now.

"He should be a couple minutes' walk away," I tell the others, and we trudge our way towards the dot immediately.

A small shack comes into sight, in the same location as the little red Mario.

This must be it.

Without having to use words, we all know the drill. I hand out the weapons, a pistol each and we silently stalk closer and closer to the cabin. It's the only thing around here, apart from us and the tumble-weed. The bleating of distant sheep and the wind whispering down our ears are the only sounds.

"Surely he can't be here?" Stefano whispers.

"It's best to make sure," I reply.

We scope the building, creeping around its edges and peeking through windows when possible, though most of them are boarded shut with wooden planks. We'll have to go through the front door.

Stefano and Sonny are on one side, me on the

other. I count down from three on my fingers and I kick the door wide open. There's a ruckus coming from inside that makes us all stiffen, but eventually a flurry of chickens scatters out into the surrounding nature and we all breathe a sigh of relief.

Regaining focus, we head inside. It's dark and smells like shit, not unusual in a place like this. I look down at the tracker again; we're right next to it. I push my head to the side, signalling to the others that it must be around the dishevelled brick wall. I go first, wanting to be the one that shoots him if he is here.

With my pistol straight out in front of me, I swing around the corner, but what I'm greeted with is not what I ever expected.

A dead man. Tied to a chair, and badly beaten. A phone attached to his chest with chicken wire.

"Is it Mario?" Sonny asks, joining me to ogle at the scene.

"I... I don't know," I stutter.

She nudges me. "Well, go and find out."

I take a few steps closer, the smell getting worse now, and the cloud of black flies pelting my face like hail is no help at all. I use one finger, as little surface area as possible, to tilt the victim's chin up to get a better look at the face.

His hair is dark and slicked back, like Mario's. His lips are full and surrounded by a small brush of stubble, like Mario.

I wince. "I really can't tell, his face is so messed up."

"It looks like him," Sonny adds.

"About seventy percent of Italians look like him," Stefano protests.

Sonny comes to take a closer look and notices

something white sticking out of his trouser pocket. Upon inspection, it's a note written in Italian, which she reads aloud,

"*Catch me if you can, chickens.*" She looks up at us now. "He's playing with us."

"How are we going to know where to go from here?" Stefano asks, as always, the voice of reason and reality.

"Maybe we should inform the villagers. They might know him, or more importantly, if Mario was with him."

We head back into the market and we speak to the first person we come across, an old man with a long white beard, his bald head protected by a shabby straw hat.

"Does anybody live in the shack over there?" I ask him in Italian.

"Lives there? No, but my friend's son owns it, we've not heard from him in a few days, though."

"What does he look like?" Sonny asks this time.

"He has dark hair, stubble, not much to say about him, he keeps to himself."

I look around awkwardly. "We found a body in there. Sounds like who you're describing."

His face turns into a twist of horror. "I must tell his family!"

He runs off in another direction without saying any more to us.

A moment or so later, we hear a shriek. Much like the one my mother formed through the phone, or when Calvino was killed. A young woman and an older man come dashing past us from the village towards the shack.

Once the dust, and the man's family, has settled

enough, we send Sonny over to talk to the woman, who's sitting on her own on a stone wall,

"Did you know him?" she asks, posing naivety.

"He was my brother." She sniffs, wiping her eyes with a white handkerchief.

"Oh, I'm so sorry."

She blows her nose into the cloth loudly.

"What's his name?"

She blinks the tears away. "Aldo."

"Do you know who could've done this?"

"I don't know." She weeps. "My neighbour told me that they were robbed, and that they took my brother."

"Who's your neighbour?"

"I don't really know him," she starts, but her father joins them by the wall now and, even from this distance, I can see she's scared of him, so she stops in her tracks.

Sonny picks up on this and asks an easier question. "What's your name?"

"Maria."

17

———

MARIO

"Hey, Salva, can I borrow your brother?" I ask him, hanging out of the back door.

He frowns, the midday sun shining in his eyes. "Borrow him? For what?"

"I'm just nipping into the market, thought he might like to get outdoors."

I can tell by the way he's looking at me that he doesn't trust me, which is clever on his part. A nuisance for me, though.

"He doesn't like it there, it's too busy. Plus, he doesn't want people looking at him," he tells me, resting his ice-cold drink on the table.

I shrug. "That's fair. I wouldn't even want to own a mirror if I looked like him." I laugh.

He scowls.

I give up trying to reason with him and head back inside. Matteo is sitting alone in the living room, his wheelchair facing the window so he has some entertainment. I crouch down next to him to see what the view is like and, as suspected, it's boring. Nothing but sky.

He must be losing his mind.

"Wanna get out of here, Matteo?" I ask him slowly, like a child.

He makes a noise in response and shakes his head from side to side as much as he possibly can.

"Yeah?"

"Mno!" he mumbles through stapled lips.

"Okay, okay, stop nagging me. I'll take you to the market."

He starts shouting now, guttural sounds, as I begin wheeling him towards the door.

"Mario, what are you doing?" Bella asks, floating down the stairs in her sundress.

"I'm taking Matteo to the market," I reply coolly.

She spins Matteo around to face her,

"Do you want to go?" she asks sympathetically.

He must've told her 'no' in his own little way, because she forcefully pulls him away from me,

"He doesn't want to. He can come and sit outside with us instead."

He relaxes now, as he is wheeled to safety by the beautiful goddess that is my sister. She looks angrily over her shoulder at me.

"I love you, Bella. You look beautiful, glowing." I kiss my fingers and throw them out in the air.

She ignores me.

Strange, flattery usually works on her.

I head out anyway, without anything or anyone to play with, but not for long, as Maria and some other guy in a shitty hat are doing a spot of gardening on the front path.

Surely she's not dating that loser?

She's startled to see me after the run-in with her dad.

"Mario! You cannot be seen here." She rushes over to me. "Are you okay?"

"I'm fine. But your father does know I live next door, right? He can't expect me to keep away." I spot an opening for some flirtation. "Especially not from someone as beautiful as you."

She blushes as I stroke a strand of hair away behind her ear.

"Who's this?" I nod to the guy crouched down behind her; he's been watching us this whole time.

"Oh, this is my brother, Aldo." She beams.

He stands and wipes his hand on his trousers before extending it to me. "Hello."

He looks wary of me, maybe I can use this to my advantage.

"I suppose you've heard about me?"

He nods. "Yes."

"I'm really not a bad guy, I just had too much to drink that night. You understand, right?"

"I suppose." His right shoulder raises into a shrug.

"Hey, I know." I pretend to be spontaneous. "Why don't you come to the market with me and I'll buy you a drink on the way back."

And the Best Actor Oscar goes to...

"Okay, sure." He smiles weakly.

... Mario Fontana.

"You don't mind do you, *prediletta?*" (Darling.) I flash my charming smile at Maria.

"Of course not, you can show him the farm, Aldo!"

"Oh, you have a farm down there?"

"It's more of a shack," Aldo explains, "but we have some chickens."

"Sounds perfect." I beam.

We make small talk on the way down to the farm, so I can find out a little more about Maria and her family, about how her mother isn't well. Not like I care, I just want the information.

"It's a real shame," I comment.

"It is. Maria and I are pretty much all she has left. Dad is always working, or drunk."

The side of my face twinges with the mention of their father, he's got a good punch on him.

"Was he drunk when he socked me?"

"Probably."

"Has he hit you before?"

This makes him laugh, for some reason.

"I've lost count of how many times he's hit me, or flogged me."

"Really?"

He stops in the middle of the path and rolls his trouser leg up. "Look, see this?" A giant, shiny, pink scar runs all the way down his leg. "He did that to me, with chicken wire."

"Jesus!"

We carry on walking, Aldo letting his trouser leg fall back into place on its own accord. It seems like we've teleported as the next thing I notice, we're in the middle of the bustling market, where before only the wildlife could be seen or heard.

"People must be scared of him around here," I say, looking at all the dirty peasants touching their dirty crops.

Aldo snaps a twig from a tree above our heads and he swings it around in the wind as we draw closer to the shack now.

"I suppose. They stay out of our way and us out of theirs."

Glad to hear it.

"This is it." He points to the shack in the distance with his stick.

Something unusual happens, I'm lost for words. It's a shit hole, but you can't very well tell somebody that to their face. Honestly, it's the worst place I've ever seen, it's... "Quaint," I manage to conjure up.

"What does that mean?" Aldo frowns.

I forgot I was among the uncivilised.

"It's nice." I smile, holding back my frustration at his stupidity.

"It's okay. The only nice thing Dad has ever done for me."

"Can we look inside?" I tempt.

He nods and leads the way.

The inside is even worse than it looked from afar. How this is even classed as a farm I'll never know. There's straw scattered all over the floor, broken wood everywhere, and it's full of fucking chickens.

"There's not much to see in here. We should go back, you can get me that drink you promised."

I spot something shimmering in the beams of sunlight falling through the cracks in the structure. I pick it up and see that it's a stretch of chicken wire.

"Is this the sort of thing your father used on you?"

He turns around, looking troubled. "I suppose so, why?"

I ignore his question. "I suppose he would've done something like this with it."

I swing it through the air and it whips across his face, leaving an angry red line from his forehead to his chin.

He screams out in pain and coddles the wound. "What the fuck, man!"

I swing it again and it collides with his shoulder, ripping his shirt open. He screams again, so I have to keep going to keep him quiet.

I have to keep going.

I take his shirt off before I do any more damage, though, I'll be needing that.

Once I'm sure he's dead, and unidentifiable, I tie him to the best-formed chair there is and tie my phone to his chest.

Those idiots thought I'd forget about the little trackers inside the phones I've been using for almost half my life. I don't mind leaving them a trail of bread crumbs, though, it keeps things exciting.

I write a love letter for them and put it in Aldo's pocket. Now for my master plan. I dress up in his clothes, putting his shitty little hat on, worrying about whether I'm going to contract nits from this dirty *contadino's* head. (Peasant.)

I make sure to make lots of noise, mainly by kicking a few of the chickens, before running out of the shack, looking towards the market. I see villagers looking at me – perfect – then I run towards the forest, out of sight.

Taking the long route back home, I feel like I'm on a pilgrimage, no water to drink, no proper clothes on my back, I truly am a saint, a man of God.

Maria is on the steps when I get back.

Fuck's sake

"Hello, Maria."

She gets up from the stoop, startled. "What happened to you? Where's Aldo?"

"We got robbed. They took him."

"Who took him?" She becomes frantic.

Calm down, you fucking... "Baby, it's okay. I'm sure he'll be fine. I made it back alive, didn't I?"

This doesn't seem to soothe her at all. She slaps me across the face, but it stuns me more than it hurts. She trudges back inside, probably to get her father, the big macho man that beats his son. I did them both a favour.

I head inside to clean up before the beast enters the ring with me again. I shower and change into my smartest clothes, which, regrettably, aren't as smart as I'd like, but a clean shirt will do.

Bella and Salva must've been very busy bees whilst I was out, as they have some news for me.

"We found you somewhere to live."

I join them around the table outside, trying not to look at Matteo, so he doesn't put me off the sangria I've just poured myself.

"Oh, yeah? Tell me about it."

"It's not far from here, two bedrooms, one bathroom. What more could you need?" Salva describes.

What more could I need?

"Great. When can I move in?"

Bella clears her throat elegantly, like our mother used to when she had something hurtful to say. "We moved your stuff in already."

Normally, I would not stand for this clear wish to avoid me, but it's come in handy, my guest is due to arrive any minute now.

"Even better! Care to show me where it is?"

Salva takes one for the team, apparently, and he

reluctantly walks me over to another similar building to the one they live in, in the same block of crumbling ruins.

"Enjoy," he says quickly, leaving me outside the house.

"Salva?"

He turns around slowly. "Yes?"

"I need the keys."

He looks relieved and digs them out of his pocket. "Of course." He throws them over to me. "How silly of me."

I catch them with ease and wink at him, though he doesn't seem any less wary of me.

I put the key in the lock and it feels loose and opens without any effort on my part. Inside is even worse than Salva's place, it's like they didn't even bother to clean the place up for me! *I'll call Bella later to come and sweep up.*

My belongings are waiting for me in the hall and I take what I need upstairs. I pick the biggest room for myself, obviously, though it's nothing like what I was used to at The Complex.

I should blow that place up. I'll write that down for later.

My contact tells me he's here and I hastily get ready to go and pick him up. That must mean the deed is done and I can finally begin planning my own Mafia exploits. This is going to be amazing, the best Mafia the world has ever known.

But can I use the Fontana name? I wouldn't want my father overshadowing me, I'll have to think of something else.

18

ANASTACIA

I finally come to. My throat and eyes burn and everywhere hurts, deep in my bones. I manage to peel my eyes open and I can see smoke everywhere, Roman, my pilot, dead and bloody next to me, still strapped in his seat.

How the fuck have I survived this?

I unbuckle the seatbelt and look around for an exit. I'm left with no choice, I kick the window with all my force. My shinbones splinter inside me, but the pain keeps me fighting. The glass crumbles to the floor and I drag myself out of the window, cutting my forearms badly.

Standing up is the hardest part, I swear I've broken both legs, but I need to get away from the wreck before it blows. Through a mix of crawling and limping, I make it over to a brick wall. It looks abandoned and like a war was fought here, but it's enough protection from the blast if I need it.

I rest my head against a brick poking out of the lower part of the wall and force my phone out of my pocket, to call my father.

He answers quickly. "Yes? He is dead?"

"No, we ran into some trouble, the plane crashed and I am badly hurt. I need your help."

He does not reply,

"Dad?"

"I will not help you, Anastacia, this was your mission."

"You *won't*?" I bark.

"I won't. You're on your own." He hangs up the call.

I stare out into the desert, my phone still held to my ear, my mouth still hanging open.

I thought he loved me.

The plane explodes behind me, sending shrapnel hurtling over the wall and landing in balls of flames by my feet. I look into the fire and it mimics what I'm feeling inside, just not as violent.

I *will* finish this mission, by myself, and my father *will* love me, and he *will* be proud of me!

Suddenly, all my pain goes away, and I stand erect and strong like nothing ever happened. I tuck my gun back into its holster, thankfully still intact.

I try to flag people down on my walk towards the village but nobody will stop for me. Finding a piece of broken metal on the floor, I use it as a mirror and *oh my God,* no wonder nobody wants to pick me up. My hair is now red with blood and my face is barely distinguishable. My clothes are torn and I walk with a double limp. They must think a zombie apocalypse is imminent, you know how the rural types can be superstitious.

I'll just have to drag myself the whole way there, even if I don't know exactly where I'm going.

A few miles from our crash site, I see something smouldering, another plane crash, still fresh. Déjà vu? A mirage? I go in to take a closer look.

It's the Fontanas' plane, no doubt, but nobody is inside. There's no sign that they were ever here, no blood or footprints in the dirt.

Suddenly, I get the most amazing thought; *why don't I call Maria?*

In all my haste, I forgot how I ended up here in the first place!

I dial her instantly. "Maria. I need you to pick me up," I order her.

"I can't," she snivels, "my brother has been killed, my father arrested, I can't leave my mother."

"Fuck your mother! Pick me up now! Now! Now! Now!"

"I will not help you any more, you monster! Mario is good man."

I scoff loudly. "Oh, yeah? He told you that?"

"I know it myself."

"You don't know dick! I bet he killed your brother. If you come and get me, I will avenge him for you."

"Anastacia..." she says calmly, "you are sad girl, I understand."

"I'm not sad, Maria, I'm fucking livid! I need to get into your village now. I'm badly hurt."

"I will not help you."

"*OHHHHHHH!*" I bellow out into the wasteland ahead of me. "So you're not going to help me now, either? Well, guess what? I don't need your fucking help anyway!"

"But you just asked me for..."

"I don't need your help!" I shout, before ending the call so that I get the last word over her.

Looks like I really am alone. But if I'm going down, I'm taking someone with me, and I have my sights set on the Italians.

19

SHELLEY

Sitting around Manchester airport with Bertolt doesn't half bring some weird looks. But he is oblivious and just enjoys being himself, that's what I like about him.

Don't tell him I like him.

I can't help but wish that first vision hadn't been interrupted; it's all I can think about. Turning to him, I finally ask, "Bert, can we try again?"

I try to keep my voice low, but the woman in front of us glances up from her magazine momentarily, obviously already interested in us.

He looks shocked. "Here?"

"Yeah, well... we can go into a quieter room, or maybe even the bathroom."

The woman's eyes ping-pong between me and Bert, an intrigued smirk on her face.

"Mistur Shelley, are you sure you vant to do zat?"

"I can't stop thinking about last time. It would've worked if we weren't interrupted."

The woman frowns for a millisecond, her mind working like clockwork trying to piece the conversation together.

Bert smiles devilishly. "I do have mein kit in ze bag."

"Great." I'm excited too, now. "Come on, let's go into that room over there."

The woman stares after us, wishing she could get a glimpse at whatever fetish we'll be feeding in here.

We sit on the floor, despite there being a number of chairs around a large boardroom table. It's getting harder and harder to cross my legs properly now I'm getting older and have been out of work for a while, I've noticed. *I'll have to work on that when I get home.*

"Are you ready, Mistur Shelley?"

I nod.

"Okay." He passes me the concoction to drink. "Deep breaths, remember, cloze your eyes."

I swallow it with a quick wince and shiver, almost gagging again. "It tastes different," I comment.

"Zis von ist more powerful, you vill see *everysing*. It is time."

This sends a shock of panic through my body for some reason. My eyes start to pound and it's as if my vision is being pulled into another dimension, and with some force, I must say. It all comes to me so quickly, it feels like I'm only out for ten seconds,

The murder at Paradox Park

Questioning of suspects

Al and Sonny meeting the Fontanas for the first time

The SWAT raid

The girls killing Detective Leaver

Killing so many people

My wife sat by the phone

The girls meeting Bertolt

Assassinating Holdis

Mario hanging from the window ledge
Len being sent to George Lee hospital
Mario killing his father
Al being murdered
Luca blowing up The Complex
Sonny jumping out of a plane
Len fleeing in the car
Arriving in ItalyAnother plane crashAnother predatorAnothermurderAnothermeetingoffoesAnoth-erdeath.

"Voah, voah, voah, too far, Mistur Shelley, I cannot show you ze rest."

I blink myself back into the real world and feel that my pulse is bulging out of my temples and I'm sweating horrendously.

"Why can't I see more? It can give us a better chance at winning."

"Life ist not about vinning. It is not somesing to be played viz."

I sigh. "Fuck sake, Bert, what's the point of you then?"

Anybody else would be offended, but not Bertolt. "I understand zat you are under a lot of stress, Mistur Shelley, but I am here to help, und I vill, but zere are limits."

"So, what does it all mean? How does the murder case I worked on have anything to do with this?"

"Don't you see? It ist all connected. Wizout one, ze uzzer could not have happened."

I mess around with the closely cropped carpet between my feet. "Al would've always ended up dead, wouldn't she?"

"In zis vay or anuzzer, yes."

This kills me. How can I bear the thought? There

was never anything I could do to stop my baby girl from being killed.

"Well, we should get back, wouldn't want to miss the plane," I mumble, wanting the whole ordeal to be over now.

Bert packs his stuff up and we head back into the departure lounge and sit in the same seats as before, still warm. *My arse was more naïve last time I was sat here, though.*

I feel worn out, like I've lived a thousand lives at once, which I suppose I kind of did. I run my fingers through my hair and wipe sweat from my brow with my sleeve. The woman in front is looking at me again now.

"Feeling better?" She smirks.

Bert and I look at each other.

"Vot? Vot do you talk of, you crasy lady." He flirts, and it makes her laugh.

God, it's like sitting next to Austin Powers.

"We're not..." I point between us, "we don't..."

"Ve do." He raises his eyebrows at her seductively.

I give up trying to convince her otherwise, as I know Bert won't let up on this joke of his.

"What do you do?" She leans in closer, elbows on knees, magazine closed with the page saved by a finger.

"I put him into a trance-like state, isn't zat right?" He nudges me.

"Yeah," I say, not really wanting to join in.

"Really?" She's a little too intrigued for my liking.

Bert nods, ready for a big explanation. "First, he must drink ze juices."

"The gate is open," I tell him, grabbing his arm and pulling him from the seat.

He laughs and points his thumb at me. "So dominant."

She giggles into her magazine.

As we stride down the terminal, I give him a little piece of helpful advice. "Bert, if you ever do that again, I will gladly punch you so hard in the face that you'll only be able to see it in visions."

"Oh, it's just a bit of fun, Mistur Shelley! Al found it razur hilarious."

"Well, you can tell her, from me, that it's not funny, and that she's grounded."

"Uh-ohh, Alice, sounds like you're in trouble," he says to his head.

It's almost become normal to me now, to communicate with my dead daughter through a German mystic's head. I never would've believed it, ever, but the things he says, nobody else could possibly know but Al.

It comforts me to think that she's here with me every step of the way, like I would've loved to have done for her.

20

MARIA

The police questioned us all once my brother's body was found. Italian police are not well known for being thorough investigators, so I had no hope that they would ever catch his killer, or killers.

They asked me who the last person to see Aldo was, so of course I gave them Mario's name. I sat with him as they asked him the hard-hitting questions.

"I know exactly who did it, gentlemen," he explains, to their surprise.

"*Dirci.*" (Tell us.)

"*Il Toro.*"

I gasp. "Mario, what are you saying?"

"The truth," he exclaims. "I recognised him from his sheer size, and did you notice the murder weapon was chicken wire? Maria will tell you, he's beaten his son that way before."

"Is this true?" The policeman asks.

"*Sì... però...*"

Before I can finish, the main policeman sends one of the officers to arrest my father.

"Thank you for all your help." He shakes Mario's hand like he's a hero.

When they leave, I drag Mario over to me, down the side of my house,

"Was it really my father?"

"I'm afraid so, Maria."

I almost burst into tears. "What are we going to do?" I collapse onto my knees. "I can't run the farm and look after Mama at the same time."

"I'll help you," he offers, joining me on the floor, but making sure he doesn't get his new suit dirty.

"You will?"

"Of course."

"What will you do?"

"I'll kill your mother and then you can come and live with me," he says softly.

I stare at his sincere face; I feel so terrified of him in this moment.

He breaks out into gentle laughter. "I'm joking."

It is not funny to me, though.

"I think it is best if you don't speak to me again," I tell him, and I stand up, just wishing to be away from him.

"Baby, I was joking. Maybe in poor taste, but a joke nonetheless."

"I don't want to see you again, Mario."

"Fine... Then you won't see *anything* again!" he roars.

He grabs me by the throat and pushes me against the wall behind us.

"Let me fill you in on everything you've missed," he begins, as he slowly drains me of life, "I killed people before I came here, including my own father. When I got here, I killed your brother, then framed your father. Now I'm going to kill you, and when that's done..." He pauses as my eyes start to bulge and bleed tears and my face turns a dash of blueberry.

"I'm going to kill your mother, and burn your shitty little village to the ground."

That's enough for me to let go, let my soul slip away from my body. Why should I live when there will be nothing left to live for soon?

My last thought was not about my family, or my lost future. I wished I had told Anastacia where Mario was.

21

MARIO

I don't do anything special with her body, just drag it further out of view. Nobody will care about her, anyway.

For a split second, I contemplate going upstairs to kill her mother, but there's no point in that, either; she'll do the job herself, I'm sure.

Instead, I head back to my new home, where my guest is waiting in hiding. He, too, has killed people, but he's more cautious than I am. He made me *promise* not to tell anybody he's here. My promises don't mean anything but I did it anyway, just to appease him.

He's upstairs in the spare bedroom. I knock on the door and he calls for me to come in.

"Want to watch the football?" I ask him. "It's just starting."

"Who's playing?"

"Milan versus Juventus."

He gets up off the bed. "Yeah!"

22

SONNY

"Do you know where Maria lives?" I ask one of the locals.

He just points rather than tells me where she lives, so we end up walking in the general direction the man told us to go.

Every house looks exactly the same, anyway; it'd be like playing *Guess Who?*, where the only characters are shadows.

As we walk further, I ask everyone we pass where Maria lives, and we finally start getting closer as people throw their finger *over* buildings, meaning it should be on the next street.

When we get there, there are two houses in closer proximity to each other than the rest.

"Maybe we should check these out," Stefano reckons.

He has a feeling for these things.

We check the front windows of the house on the right first. Nothing moves inside, but I can see food left out on the table, and a cigarette, still spilling smoke, is left teetering on the edge of a bowl, a long trail of ash threatening to cover the wooden tabletop.

"I'll go around the back," I whisper to the guys.

I sneak down the side of the house, making sure not to step on anything that might alert somebody. Beneath my shoe I feel something hard, but it makes doesn't make the loud noise I was expecting.

I look down and see it's a hand I've stood on. I remove the layer of shrubs covering the body. It's a woman. I don't recognise her, but I can tell she used to be beautiful when she was alive. It looks as if she's been strangled. *Definitely Mario's doing.*

I look around the floor for evidence, there's nothing of significance. Then I hear a familiar laugh come from over the other side of the fence. I scour it for a small hole to peep through, which I find further into the garden of the house.

Just as I expected. Salva and Bella.

My heart stops when I see her. It was so long ago. *None of that matters now.*

I head back to the front of the house and inform Luca and Stefano of my find.

"This must be Maria," Luca says, looking over the body. "She said she lived next to someone who told her about her brother's death."

"You think Mario lives there?"

"Let's find out."

We let ourselves into the unlocked front door. *You think they'd be more careful.* There's a man in a wheelchair, sitting on his own in the living room. He looks very startled to see us and he desperately tries to manoeuvre himself out of his chair.

"It's okay, we won't hurt you." I try to calm him down.

"Fuck me," Luca says out of nowhere.

I turn to face him. "What's up?"

"It's Matteo."

"Are you sure?"

"I'm positive! Look, he always wears that ring."

Sure enough, this signature ring is on his finger.

We decide Matteo can come with us to surprise his two landlords.

I push him out of the door first and Salva is the first to notice us. He gets out of his chair so fast that it's thrown across the garden. He instinctively puts his hand where his pistol would usually be kept.

Bella stands now, too. She doesn't take her eyes off me.

"What are you doing here?" Salva asks, trying to sound aggressive but we can hear the panicked notes.

"I think you know," Luca replies.

"He's not here!" he protests.

"Then where is he?"

"We don't know." Bella answers this time.

She's always been a good liar, but not good enough.

"Okay..." I pull out my pistol and hold it to Matteo's head.

I know what you're thinking. I've changed. I would never threaten an innocent, defenceless man. But trust me, I have no intention of killing him because I know Salva will protect his brother.

"He's a few houses down! Please, don't kill him."

Bella drops into her seat. A brother for a brother. *Their relationship won't last long after this.*

"Thanks." I smile and we all leave.

Salva rushes over to his brother and takes him back inside. It's like Bella doesn't even exist. I would never have treated her like this.

23

SHELLEY

"Alright, Bert, lead the way," I tell him, once we arrive in Italy.

"Follow me!" he sings, skipping into the warm breeze.

I hadn't realised we were going to walk the entire way, otherwise I would've put better shoes on.

He sings these German songs the whole way there and it takes a lot of effort not to tell him to shut up. Even the twins weren't *this* annoying, not even as small children.

"Mistur Shelley!" He stops in shock.

"What, what is it?" I worry.

"How dare you call me annoying." He smiles slightly and continues walking.

I can't help but smirk at him.

I can't believe my own daughter is snitching on my thoughts!

"I can!" Bert shouts over his shoulder.

Right, that's it, I'm not thinking anymore.

"Ve are almost zere, Mistur Shelley... Sumsing ist not right, zough."

"What's not right?"

He puckers his lips and looks around for his wild signs of knowledge,

"Someone ist about to beat us to it."

"We can't let that happen! I need to be the one to kill him." I rush past him, before realising he's the navigator. "Come on, Bert, we need to run."

"Oh, I love running!" He catches up to me in no time and runs ahead of me, with his finger pointing out in front of him.

"Zis is it," he whispers.

We both stand there for a while, looking up at the old brick farmhouse.

"Vot's the plan?"

"I thought you knew everything."

"I can't know vhat you don't know."

I take a deep breath. "Let's just go in quietly, and scope the place. Have you got a gun?"

"*Nein,* how am I supposed to get a gun srough ze *flughafen?*" (Airport.)

"Here." I pass him a spare pistol, but he refuses,

"Zis ist my veapon." He taps his temple like he always does.

"Suit yourself."

I slowly pry open the front door, and straight away I can hear floorboards creaking upstairs. Just to be safe, though, I do a quick sweep of the downstairs whilst Bert waits by the front door.

When I get back, he's gone. *What the fuck, Bertolt?*

I decide to leave it, and head to my target, this is more important. I check the first room; nothing. I creep over the landing and towards the final room at the front of the house. The door is ajar.

As I peek through the crack, something hits me on the back of the head and I fall to the floor unconscious, taking the door with me. When I come to, I'm tied to a chair, and so are four other people. Bertolt, Luca Fontana, another associate and...

"*Sonny!*" I scream.

I get another blow to the head for that.

"That's right," the voice behind my ear says. "After this, I'll have killed both your daughters."

I turn my pounding head to the side and Len's face is so close to mine that all I can focus on are his blue eyes.

"Len," I mumble.

"And Mario!" He introduces himself, his giant ego not letting him go unnoticed.

We're all positioned in a circle, looking in at each other. Sonny looks at me with eyes so sad it makes me want to die, which I probably will anyway.

"Well, well, well, what a lovely reunion this is," Mario goads, walking around the circle.

"Who are these people?" Len asks. "And why are they here?"

Mario goes on to describe everybody at length, revelling in his spotlight.

"And these two people here, Len, are the father and sister of your little girlfriend."

Len's jaw can be seen clenching through his tight skin, though I don't know the reason for it.

"So, who shall we kill first?" Mario invites.

"What about this guy?" Len points to Stefano. "He's the biggest."

"Great choice, it will be a nice start."

I don't know how he's done it, but Bert's managed to free himself,

"Hallo, I have a surprise for you." He smiles widely.

Mario is about to shoot him when Bert throws something on the ground that erupts into a cloud of smoke.

It feels as if time has slowed down. Every movement takes ten times the effort, like trying to run in water. The room has a blue mist from the smoke and in the middle of the circle, from the mist, appears Al.

Everybody stops in their tracks. I can't see them, but I can, I don't know how to explain it.

"Al?" I can hear Len stutter in fear.

"Hello again." Her voice is like the smoke itself; you can hear it, but it's not there. If you wave your hand through it, it'll dissipate for good. "You'll be interested to know, I've spoken to Flic."

"What?" He really starts to panic now.

"She wants you to be as dead as we are."

Al turns to Mario now. "And YOU." The word echoes through the room and the walls shake with the anger.

Mario recoils a little, but tries to stand tall. "The Don is coming for you."

A gunshot blasts our eardrums and the smoke begins to fade.

Luca is out of his seat, his pistol shaking in his hand. Len panics and tries to run out of the door. Bert unties me quickly and I, too, get to avenge my family. One shot to the back and Len goes tumbling over the banister and down the stairs in the most dramatic fashion.

I rush to the top of the stairs and shoot him once more, for luck.

I head back into the room and see that Bert has untied everybody now. I give Sonny the biggest hug I've ever given anyone. I stroke her hair and grip onto her. "I'm never letting you go again." I sort of laugh through my tears of relief.

"Good," she replies.

"My job here ist done." Bert nods with a smile and a bow.

We have a group hug before he leaves,

"Thanks for everything, Bert, I appreciate it more than you'll ever know."

"I know." He nods. Al's already told him.

"What do you plan on doing now?" Sonny asks him.

He shrugs. "Me and Al are going for a holiday." He looks up to the ceiling. "She says it vos nice to see you again, but don't make a habit of it."

Sonny and I laugh, but can't think of what to say.

Bert leaves soon after.

Sonny introduces me to Luca and Stefano; they're alright guys, I have to say. That Luca seems very bright, it's a shame he's wasting his expertise on the Mafia.

My phone ringing interrupts our meeting. "Sorry, I need to take this." I answer, it's Reinhold. "Hey, I have great news! Len is dead, and so is Mario."

He asks me a million questions that I don't have time to answer right now, so I hastily end the conversation.

"What now, Luca?" Sonny asks.

"We begin again."

"You're starting a new Mafia?" I enquire.

Sonny rolls her eyes. "Dad, please."

"Because if you are... I'll have no choice but to join you."

They all look surprised. "Really?"

"There's no going back to the force now! Plus, I have to admit, missions are so much more fun when there are no rules."

Luca extends his hand to me. "Welcome to the family."

I grasp his hand firmly and we shake on it.

Sonny holds her arm out towards the door, prompting us to leave. "Shall we?"

"We shall," I reply, knowing that's how Al would've answered.

We head outside and the warm breeze is heaven on my tired skin. Life seems to have a new feeling. The sky is brighter, the trees more beautiful, the flowers more colourful. I finally feel content, like there's now room for happiness and excitement inside of me again. I'll ring Karen when I get home, maybe we can work things out. Or maybe I'll find myself a hot new Mafia wife. I know Al would find that hilarious.

24

ANASTACIA

I begin to lose hope. I've dragged myself along the dirt for hours and haven't seen anything other than wilderness and shitty villages. I try to stick to the edge of the trees so I'm not spotted. I'm like an injured lioness that cannot give up the hunt.

Coming to the end of a small forest, I spot my prey at last. More than that, a whole herd. I don't even know who the others are, but I'll kill them anyway.

They look happy, unaware of my presence. I stalk them, waiting for the right moment to pounce. *Not yet.* A twig snaps beneath me, they're facing in my direction, can smell my scent downwind. Finally, they begin to walk away, together, in a line down the path. One pair with arms around each other, the other two standing tall with honour.

I drag myself into position, hidden underneath the tangled shrubs. I line them all up in my scope, it's easy pickings today, отца. (Father.)

He will love me.

In one swift movement, it takes mere seconds, I have fulfilled my duty. I have no intention of claiming my prize – hanging their heads above my fireplace with the bears and the deer with giant antlers. Their time is over now, a new pride is arising.

Some may say it's cowardice to shoot an unknowing person in the back. But I say it's Victory.

25

———

FINAL

The bodies of the remaining Fontana Mafia have been discovered in a quiet farming town on the outskirts of Milan, alongside those of an ex-detective, his daughter, and escaped convict Len Moscow.

Two other Mafia members have been arrested on suspicion of murder, one being Bella Fontana, the other, her lover, Salvadore Russo. Russo's brother Matteo was also apprehended, but due to his ill health, has been taken to a secure hospital instead.

Now the Mafia war is well and truly over, but police request continued surveillance as they worry something even worse may be around the corner.

I was born on the 13th of September, 1999 in Warrington, England.

I wrote this, my first book, when I was eighteen, based around my experiences in the summer of 2018.

I study linguistics at Manchester Metropolitan University, I am interested in pursuing forensic linguistics and have an interest in acquisition.

I love music, it's always been a big part of my life, as well as helping me to establish a positive attitude towards anything. Films are another love of mine, which I try to reflect in my writing style, since I generally picture my stories as films playing out in my head, which helps me to imagine what I would want to see happen next, if it really were a film.

I'm very inquisitive and want to know everything about everything. I love learning and experiencing new things and I can't wait to see where that takes me, especially in my new writing career.

To learn more about Isobel Wycherley and discover more Next Chapter authors, visit our website at www.nextchapter.pub.

Don's Vendetta
ISBN: 978-4-82414-432-4
Mass Market

Published by
Next Chapter
2-5-6 SANNO
SANNO BRIDGE
143-0023 Ota-Ku, Tokyo
+818035793528

8th June 2022